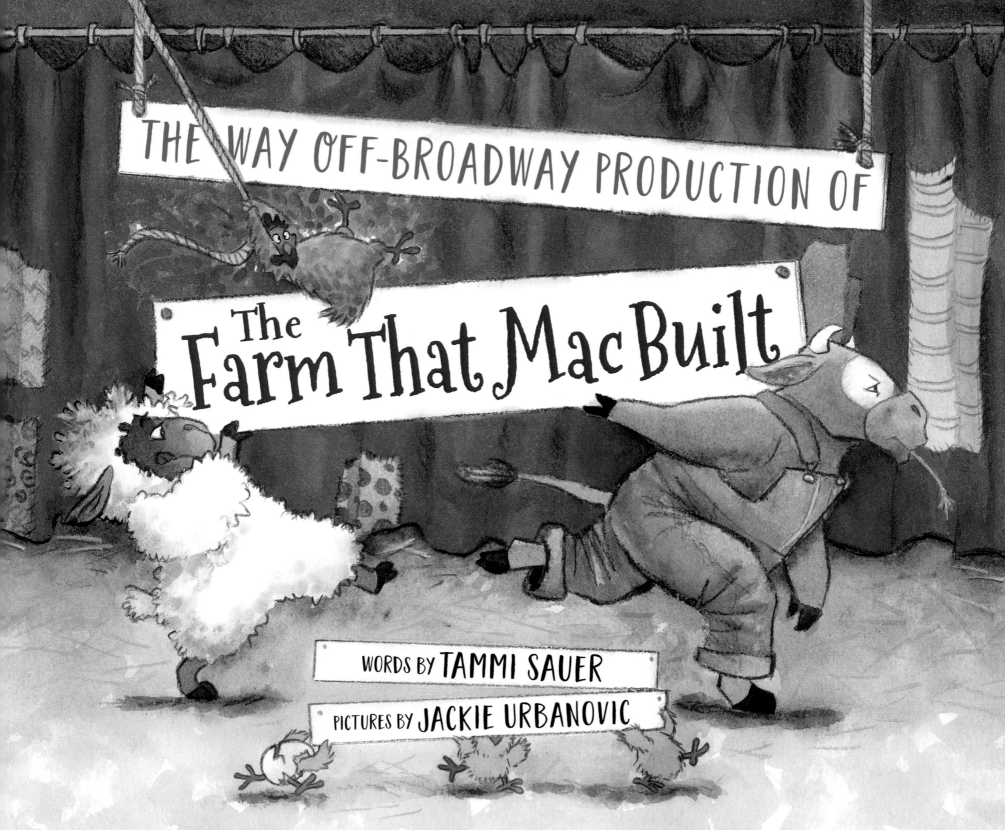

THE WAY OFF-BROADWAY PRODUCTION OF

The Farm That Mac Built

WORDS BY TAMMI SAUER

PICTURES BY JACKIE URBANOVIC

Clarion Books | Houghton Mifflin Harcourt | Boston New York

CLARION BOOKS
3 Park Avenue, New York, New York 10016

Clarion Books is an imprint of
Houghton Mifflin Harcourt Publishing Company.

hmhbooks.com

The illustrations in this book were done in watercolor and colored pencils.
The text was set in ITC Esprit Std.

Library of Congress Cataloging-in-Publication Data
Names: Sauer, Tammi, author. | Urbanovic, Jackie, illustrator.
Title: The farm that Mac built / words by Tammi Sauer ; pictures by Jackie Urbanovic.
Other titles: At head of title: The Way Off-Broadway Production of
Description: Boston ; New York : Clarion Books, Houghton Mifflin Harcourt, [2020]
Summary: The scarecrow from Old MacDonald's farm narrates an Animal Theater production of
"The House that Jack Built," but animals that do not belong on a farm keep upstaging him.
Identifiers: LCCN 2019016189 (print) | LCCN 2019018978 (ebook)
ISBN 9780544113138 (E-book) | ISBN 9780544113022 (hardcover picture book)
Subjects: | CYAC: Theater—Fiction. | Scarecrows—Fiction.
Domestic animals—Fiction. | Animals—Fiction. | Humorous stories.
Classification: LCC PZ7.S2502 (ebook) | LCC PZ7.S2502 Far 2020 (print) | DDC [E]—dc23
LC record available at https://lccn.loc.gov/2019016189

Manufactured in China
SCP 10 9 8 7 6 5 4 3 2 1
4500799110

For Jason
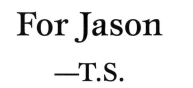
—T.S.

Hello, and welcome to Animal Theater. Today's performance is based on the mostly true story of Old MacDonald. Please sit back and enjoy the show.

THIS IS THE FARM that Mac built.
These are the . . .

. . . pigs (**Oink!**) that live on the farm
that Mac built.

These are the . . .

. . . cows (**Moo!**) that
joined the pigs (**Oink!**)
that live on the farm
that Mac built.

These are the . . .

. . . MONKEYS?!

Oh, dear. Monkeys do *not* belong on a farm.

Shoo!
Shoo!

Now, where were we? Ah, yes.

These are the . . .

. . . sheep (**Baa!**) that sprang past the cows (**Moo!**)

that joined the pigs (**Oink!**) that live on the farm that Mac built.

These are the . . .

. . . KANGAROOS?!

Heh-heh.
My apologies. *Ahem.*

This is the . . .

. . . horse (**Neigh*!***)
that pranced by the sheep (**Baa*!***)
that sprang past the cows (**Moo*!***)

that joined the pigs (**Oink*!***)
that live on the farm that
Mac built.

These are the . . .

Oh, fiddlesticks.

These are the . . .

that joined the pigs
(**Oink!**) that live on
the farm that Mac built.

Oh. I'm a bit
nervous to see
what comes next.

These are the . . .

. . . EGGS?

Yes! Eggs *do* belong on a farm.
Well done!

CRACK!

CRACK!

CRACK!

CRACK!

CRACK!

Ah, the chickies must be hatching! Let's see those cute, fluffy, yellow chickies, shall we?

PENGUINS?!

Woe is me! This is the worst barnyard play *ever*.

If only we could try again . . .

Ah, yes.
This is the farm that Mac built!

These are the chicks (**Cheep!**)
that popped from the eggs (**Crack!**)

that rolled by the chickens (**Cluck!**)
that zipped past the horse (**Neigh!**)

that pranced by the sheep (**Baa!**)

that sprang past the cows (**Moo!**)

that joined the pigs (**Oink!**)

that live on the farm that Mac built.

Thank you for being such a lovely audience. We at Animal Theater would like to wish you a wonderful rest of the day . . .